Maddie Frost
WOMBATS!
Go to Wizard's Wharf

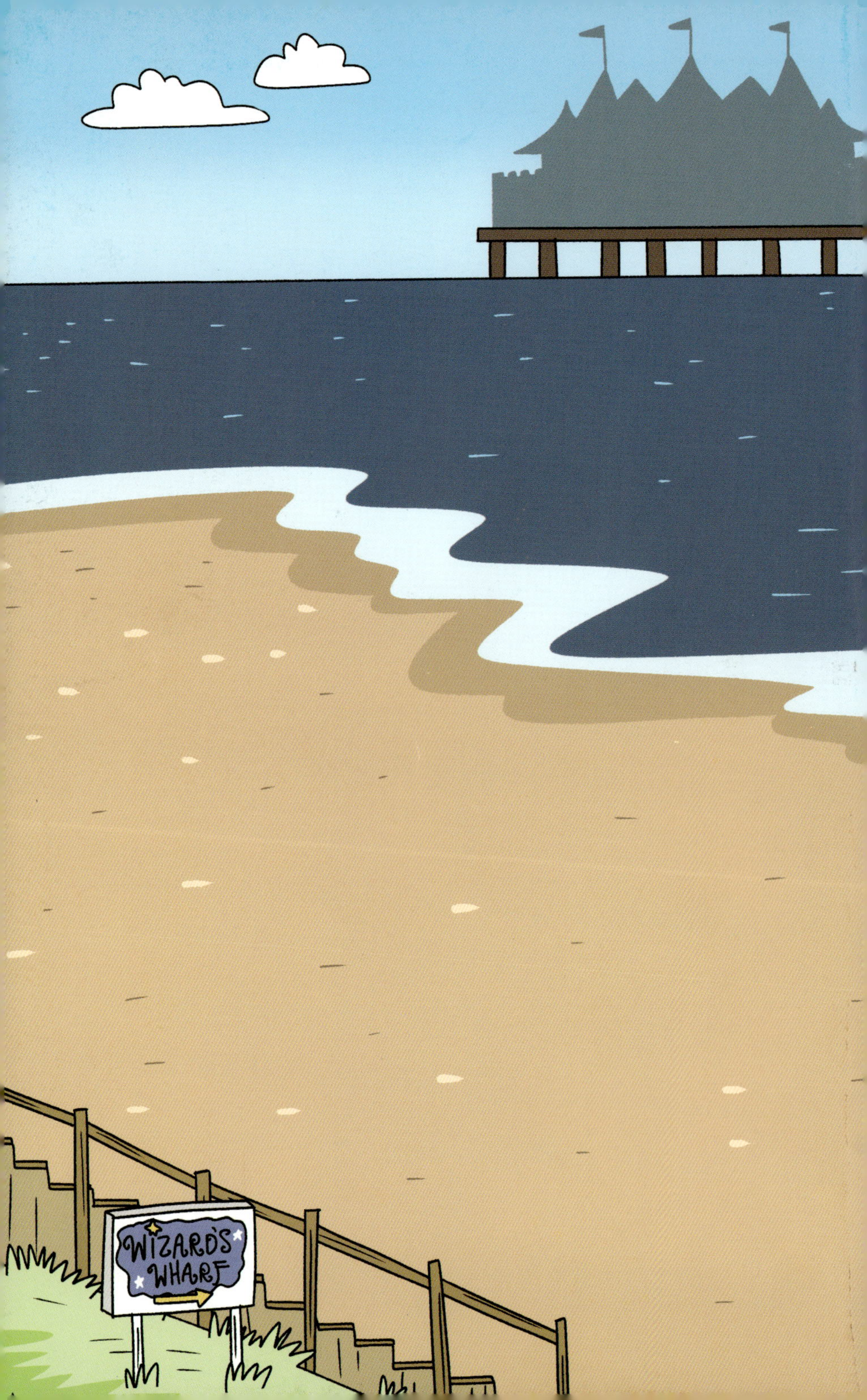
WIZARD'S WHARF

To Aneeka.
Working with you is magical.

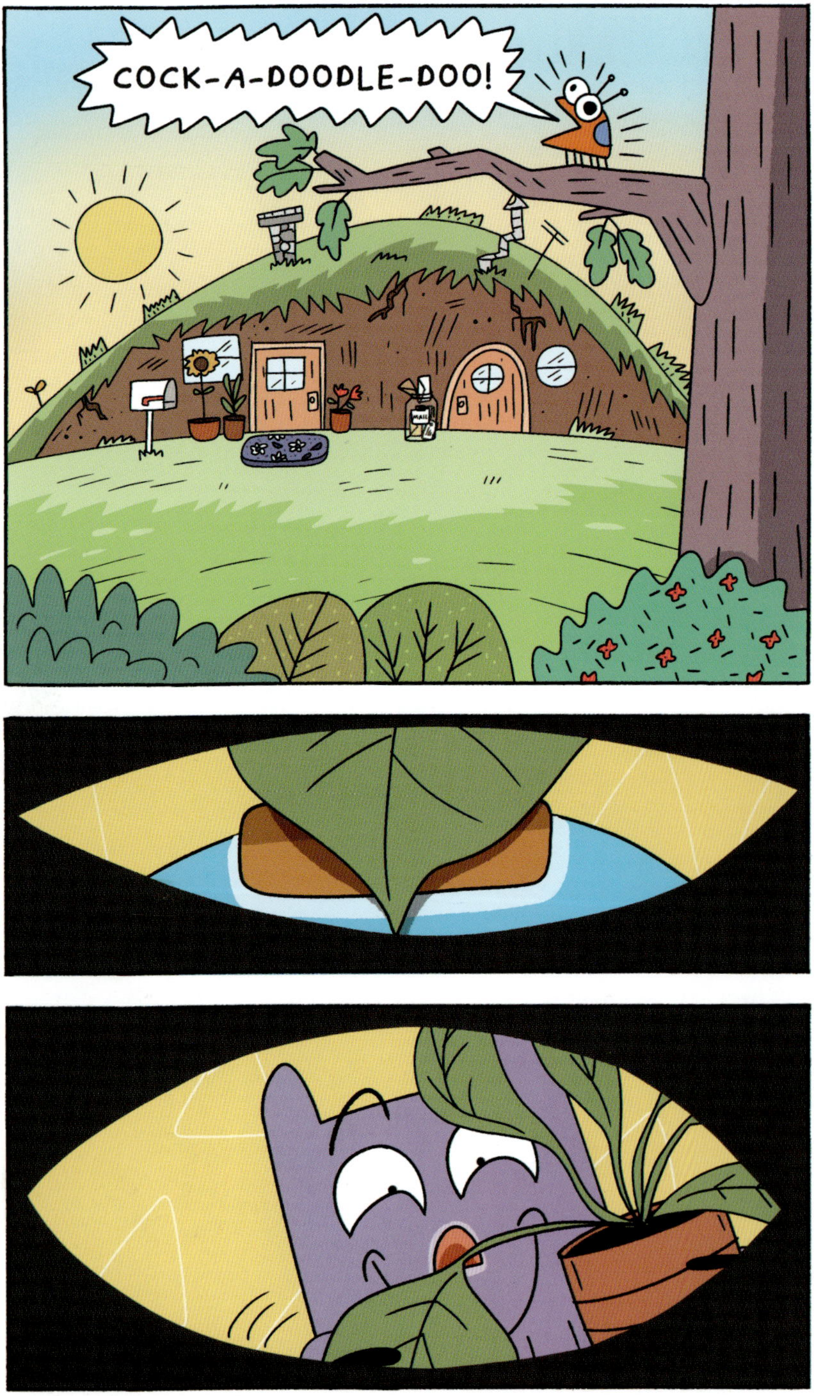
COCK-A-DOODLE-DOO!

Good morning, bestieeee.
TICKLE
TICKLE
What time is it?
Why is there a house-plant in my face?
I couldn't find a feather and needed to wake you up!
You could have just... Never mind.

Guess what today is!
Ummm...
Guess! Guess! Guess!
Saturday?
Annnnnd...
Trash day.
Nope.

National Pickle Day?
IT IS?!
Wait a minute. That's not for another three months.
AGENDA
WHOA, do NOT scare me like that.
Today isssssss...

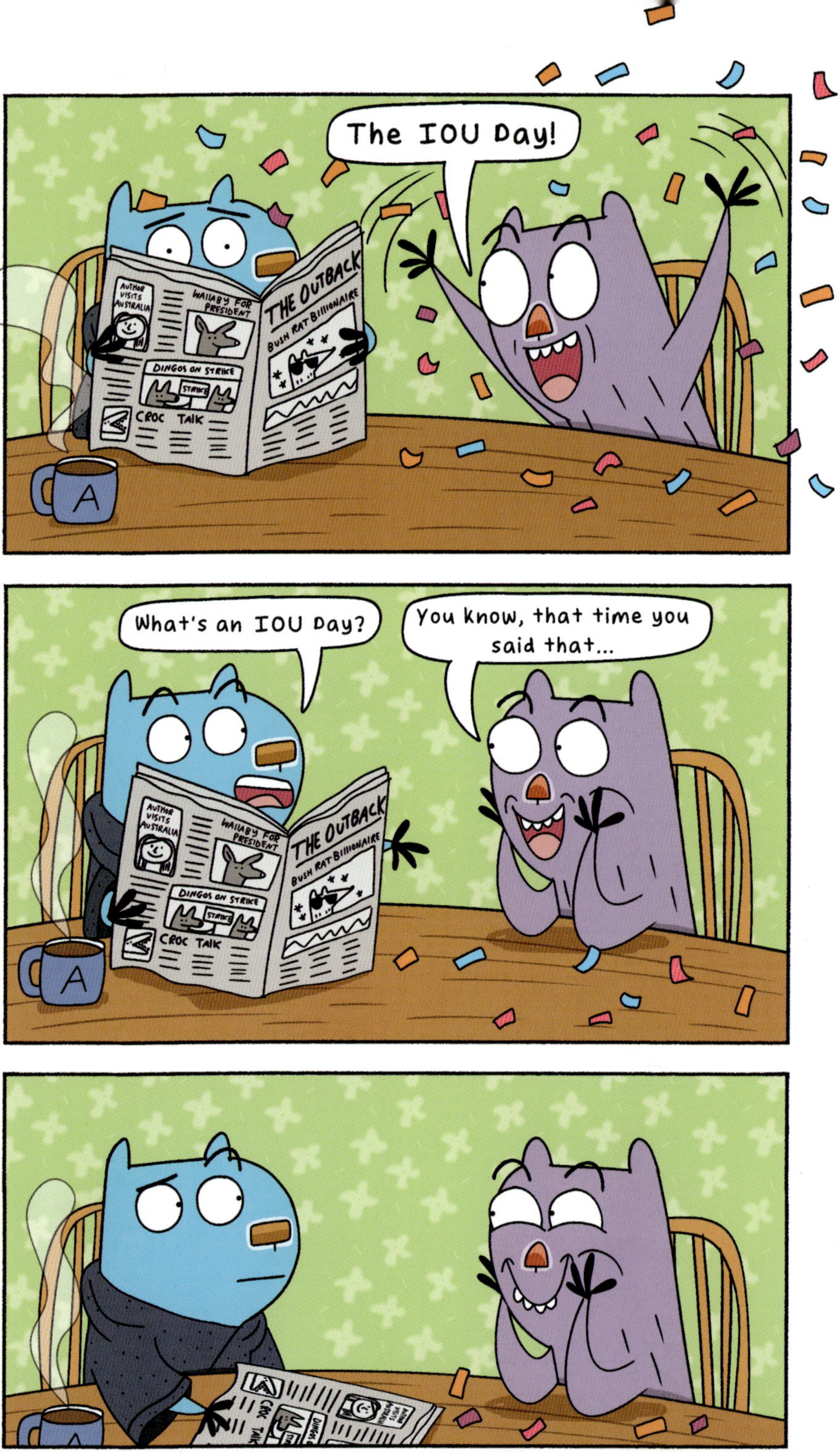
AUTHOR VISITS AUSTRALIA
WALLABY FOR PRESIDENT
THE OUTBACK
BUSH RAT BILLIONAIRE
DINGOS ON STRIKE
STRIKE
CROC TALK
The IOU Day!
What's an IOU Day?
You know, that time you said that...

Four years ago you were baking blueberry muffins and asked if I could spare an egg...
Hey, Pickles, can you spare an egg?
Sure!
And then you said...
Thanks, pal. I owe ya one!
MAIL

So today I would like to use my IOU and go to...
WIZARD'S WHARF!
Pickles, I meant "I owe you one" like a blueberry muffin. Not an entire day of funtivities.

Pleeeeeee--
eeeeeeeeeeeeeeeeee--
eeeeeeeeeeeee--
eeeeeeeeeeease?
Fine.
Hooray!
And look at that!
You're already wearing a robe.

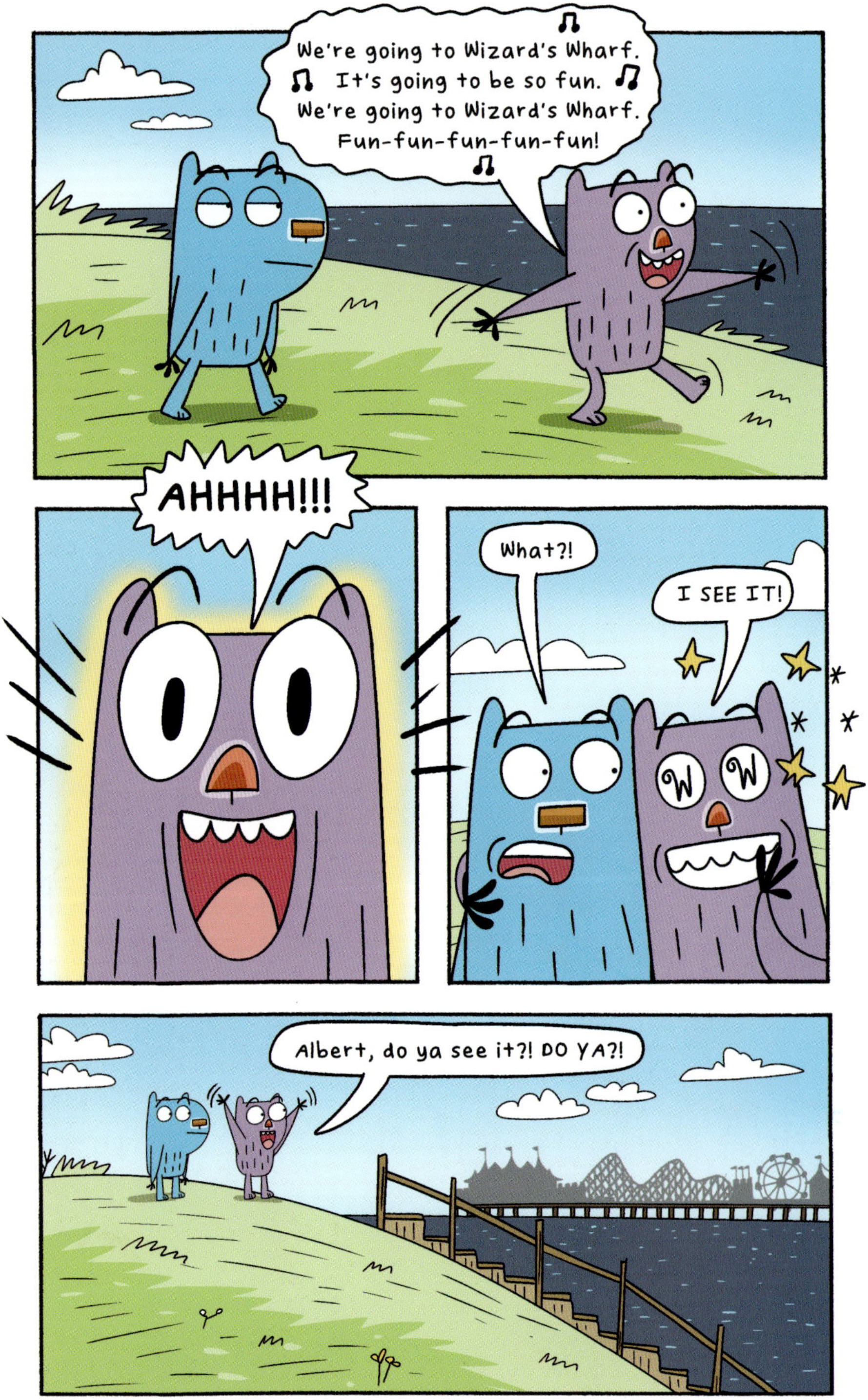
We're going to Wizard's Wharf.
It's going to be so fun.
We're going to Wizard's Wharf.
Fun-fun-fun-fun-fun!
AHHHH!!!
What?!
I SEE IT!
Albert, do ya see it?! DO YA?!

I see it.
Ohhh-kay, what's the matter, Cranky McCrank Pants?
WIZARD'S WHARF
I'm happy you're excited. It's just...theme parks aren't really my thing.
But it's such a magical place!
Don't you believe in magic?

Not really.
GASP!
So you don't believe in fairies?
Or majestic wizards?
Or magic castles?!
WHAT?!

Sorry, no.
WHAT?!
Well, mark my birds, you will after today. I guarantee it, buddy boy.
WIZARD'S WHARF NOW OPEN
This will be the most magical day EVER!

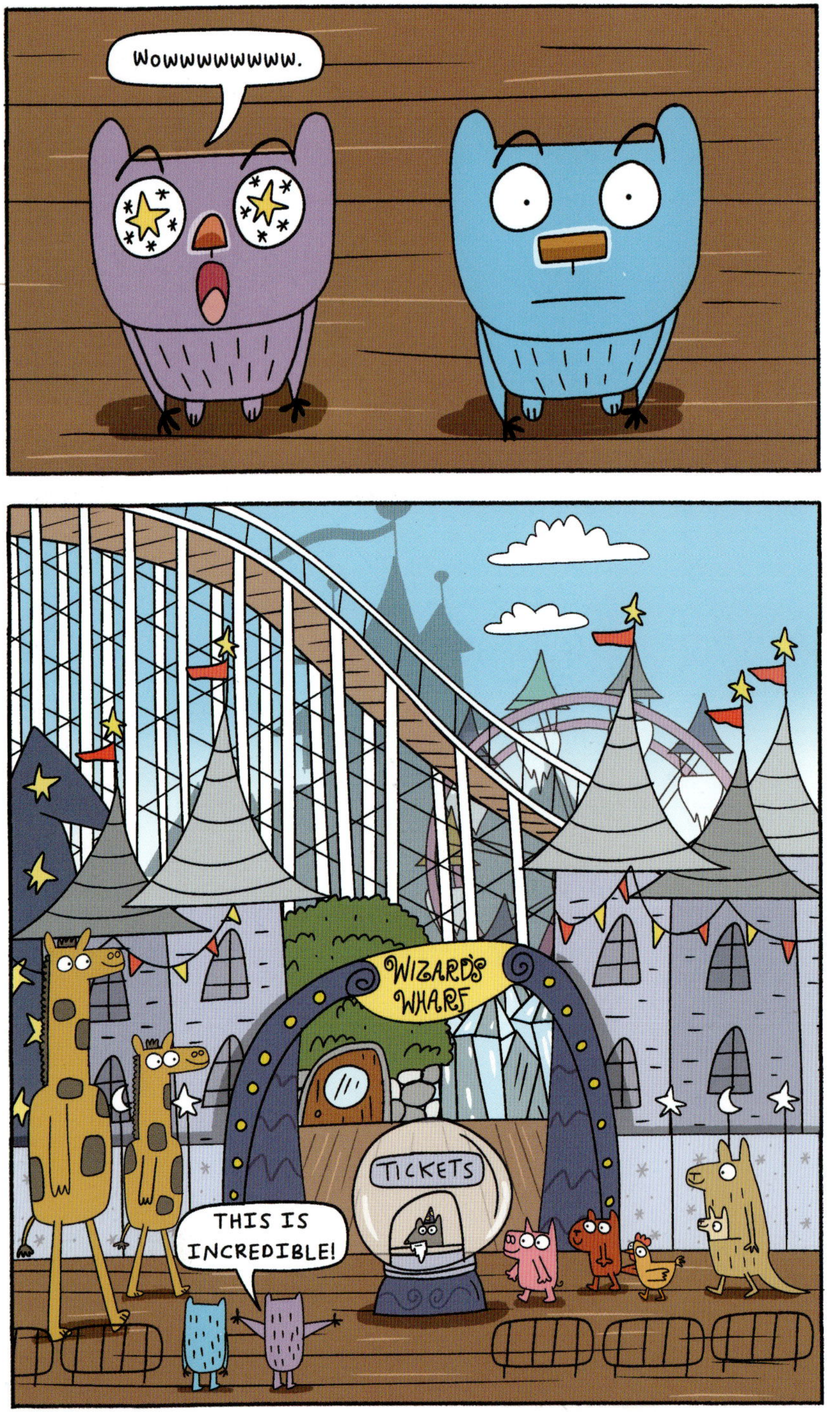
WOWWWWWWWW.
WIZARD'S WHARF
TICKETS
THIS IS INCREDIBLE!

C'mon, let's get in line for tickets.
Wait!
What?
I'm taking it all in.
Let me know when you're done.
Are you done?
Not yet.

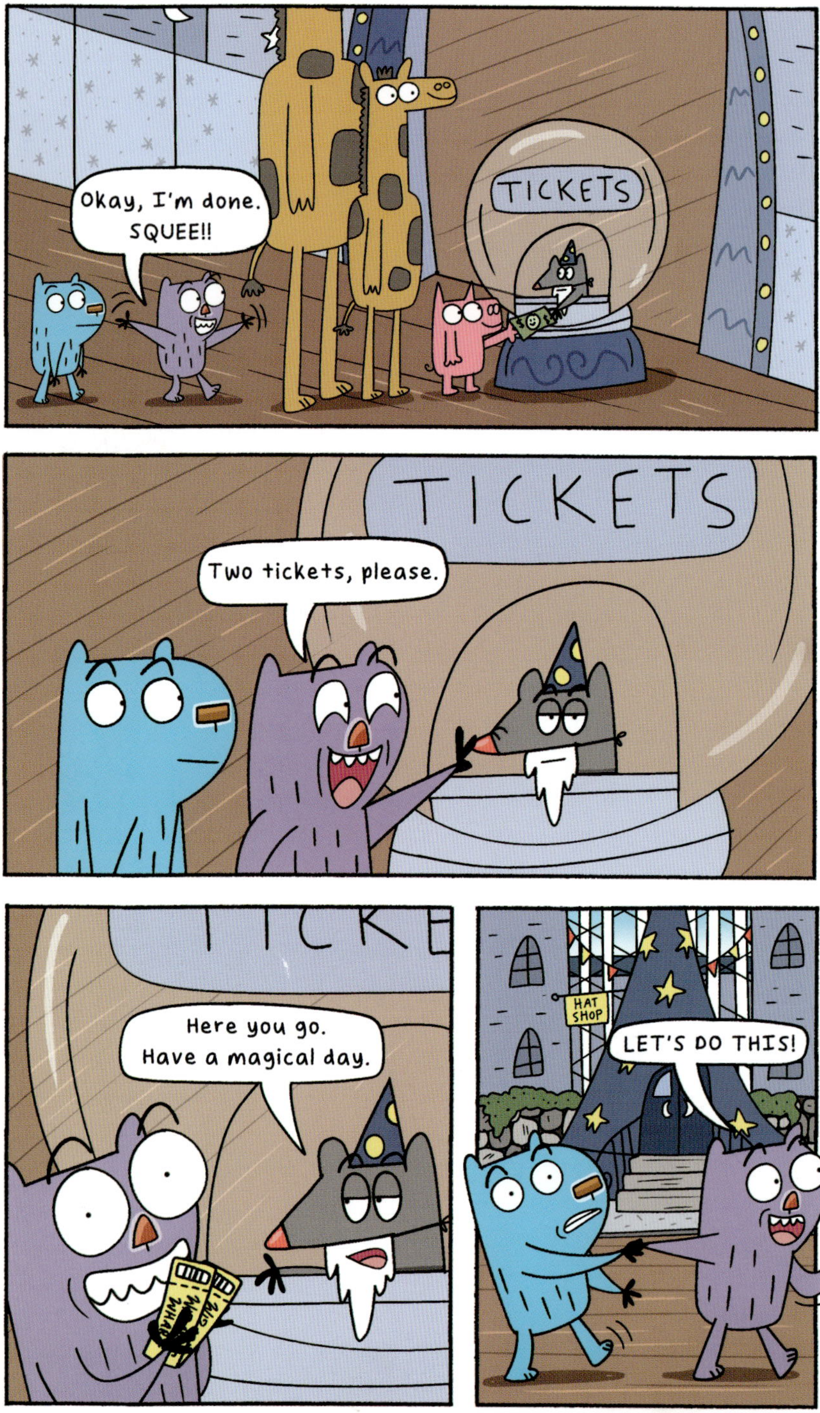
TICKETS
Okay, I'm done. SQUEE!!
TICKETS
Two tickets, please.
Here you go. Have a magical day.
HAT SHOP
LET'S DO THIS!

MUSHROOM TOSS
Soup Cauldron
HOBBIT HOUSE OF COFFEE
GIFTS
This place is awesome!
Albert, look! I'm a wizard.
Ooh, we're creepy goblins.
Yay! Fairy mice. High-five!
PHOTO OP!

Look at these games!

GEM SMASH

And rides!

WHIMSY WHIP

FAIRY GLITTER PRETZELS

HOT DOGS

MENU
HOT
XTRA HOT
PIPING
ON FIRE
BURNT

And food standssss.

Oh my gosh, Albert! A talking tree!
MAGIC TALKING TREE
Hello, majestic tree. What is your name? I'm Pickles. And that's Albert. We're having an IOU Day. Do you know what that is?
Welcome to Wizard's Wharf. Enjoy your visit, and don't forget to visit the gift shop for 20 percent off.
Well, there's nothing more magical than a sale!
MAGIC TALKING TREE
Are you ready?
For what?

FUN!
Ooh, a crystal maze!
I bet we'll be stuck in here forever.
CRYSTAL MAZE
ENTER
Wheeeee!
This is the best!

OH YEAH!
Bumper trolls!!
CRASH

Isn't 3D so cool, Albert?!

Potions
IN 3D
Hmmm, where to go next?
BUMP

AWWW! A wittle baby mushwoom! Are you lost? Are you looking for your mama? I could be your mama.
It's. Your. Magical. Day. Buy. One. Whimsy. Whip. Get. One. Free.
BEEP BOOP BEEP
WHIMSY WHIP BUY ONE GET ONE FREE!
A Whimsy Whip! That sounds delicious!
They really try to empty your wallet here, huh?

UNICORN RIDES
YOU MUST BE THIS TALL
Hey, want to ride a unicorn?
WAND REPAIR
POTION SHOP
GONE FOR LUNCH
100
50
100
20
10
I can win you one of these.
EYE-BALL
DUNGEON DONUTS
SPELL BOOKS
BOOK SALE!
Are you having fun yet?
WAAH!!
DONU
Be right back!

Close your eyes.
Okay, and...OPEN THEM!
You can't go to Wizard's Wharf without a wizard's hat.
BOOK SALE!
00:12
CANDLE MELT
I'm sorry, Pickles.
I wish I could enjoy this place as much as you, but it all seems so...fake.
Fake?
CANDLE MELT
MAGIC BALLOONS 25¢

These crystals are made of plastic.
BINK
The majestic tree has a power cord.
And this unicorn is a cow.
Well, what about the Wizard's Pet Shop? Those pets look real to me.
Sure, they're real. But they're also dressed up to look magical.

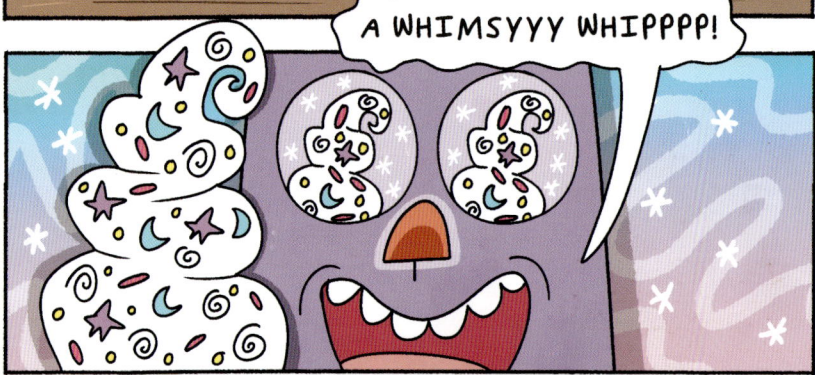

"Oh."

"Maybe this is just a bunch of, ya know...kid stuff."

"Maybe. But we're here now, so let's have fun. Okay, pal?"

"A WHIMSYYY WHIPPPP!"

Oh, Albert! You are the bestest!

Why are you eating it cone-first?

To save the best part for last!

GASP! The pegaswings!

Last one on the ride is a stinky pegasus butt.

BUMP
Oops. Pardon me.
Platters!
Hiya, Pickles.
RESTROOMS
PAY PHONE
What are you doing here?
Are you...ya know... out for another steak?
PLATTERS
•RMM•

LOOKOUT TOWER
I work here. Check it out...
PLATTERS ·RMM·
PLATTERS ·RMM
I'm saving up for a new camera. Gotta put in the time to get the dime. You smell what I'm steppin' in?
PLATTERS ·RMM·
SORCERER'S SODA
FLAVORS
FRUIT FIZZ
BLUEBERRY BUBBLE
PURPLE POP
PHOTO BOOTH
TRASH
WIZARD BEARDS
I smell popcorn.
So what exactly do you do?

YOU MUST BE THIS TALL TO RIDE THE MERRY-GO-MUSHROOMS

"RMM. Ride Mechanic Manager. I make sure all the rides are running smoothly."

CLANK

"Better tighten that later."

"Speaking of rides, you guys wanna see something totally TOP SECRET?"

YES!
Wait.
Is it scary?
CYCLOPS
ARCADE
THE GRIFFIN
GRILL
Platters?
Is it scary?
You'll have to
wait and see.
YOU MUST BE THIS TALL TO RIDE THE MERRY-GO-MUSHROOMS

"Well, wombats, whaddaya think?"

"It's the most amazing castle I've ever seen."

"This isn't just any castle..."

"It's a WIZARD'S castle."

UNDER CONSTRUCTION

TRESPASSING

UNDER CONSTRUCTION

CAUTION
CAUTION
CAUTION
CAUTION
It looks closed.
When does it open?
Not for a while.
But luckily for you two,
the door is open.
PLATTERS
·RMM·
But you can't tell anyone.
Got it?
Got it.
PLATTERS
·RMM·
Follow me.

Behold!
The wizard's castle!
Now, THIS is magical.
Don't you think, Albert?
It's cool, I guess.
So it's like a haunted house?
You walk through and things
pop out to scare you?
Things are going to pop out?

"Sort of. It's like an escape room. Or escape castle..."

"There are three wings you can explore. And it's up to you which direction you go in."

EAST WING
WEST WING
NORTH WING

"Eventually all wings lead to the exit."

"Which way is that?"

"One sec. I'm being called on my walkie-talkie."

Oh no.
CREEEAK
SLAM!
Um. Platters?
KNOCK
KNOCK
Can you open the door? It's locked.
YANK

Sorry, guys!
Wait right there. I need to get the key.
EAST WING
WEST WING
NORTH WING
We're trapped?
WE'RE TRAPPED!!!
How long will it take to get the key?
Just a few minutes. Stay right there. I'll be right back.

What do we do?
We wait.
Thank GOODNESS you got me this Whimsy Whip. Who knows when my next meal will be?
You're making a mess.
Let's look for something to clean it up. We don't want Platters getting in trouble.
SPLAT

WIPE
WIPE
I was thinking more along the lines of a mop.
Look for a utility closet.
Hmm...utility.
Utilityyy...

Util--
UTILITY!
HEY, ALBERT! I FOUND A MOP!
SMACK
And the perfect Whimsy Whip stand.

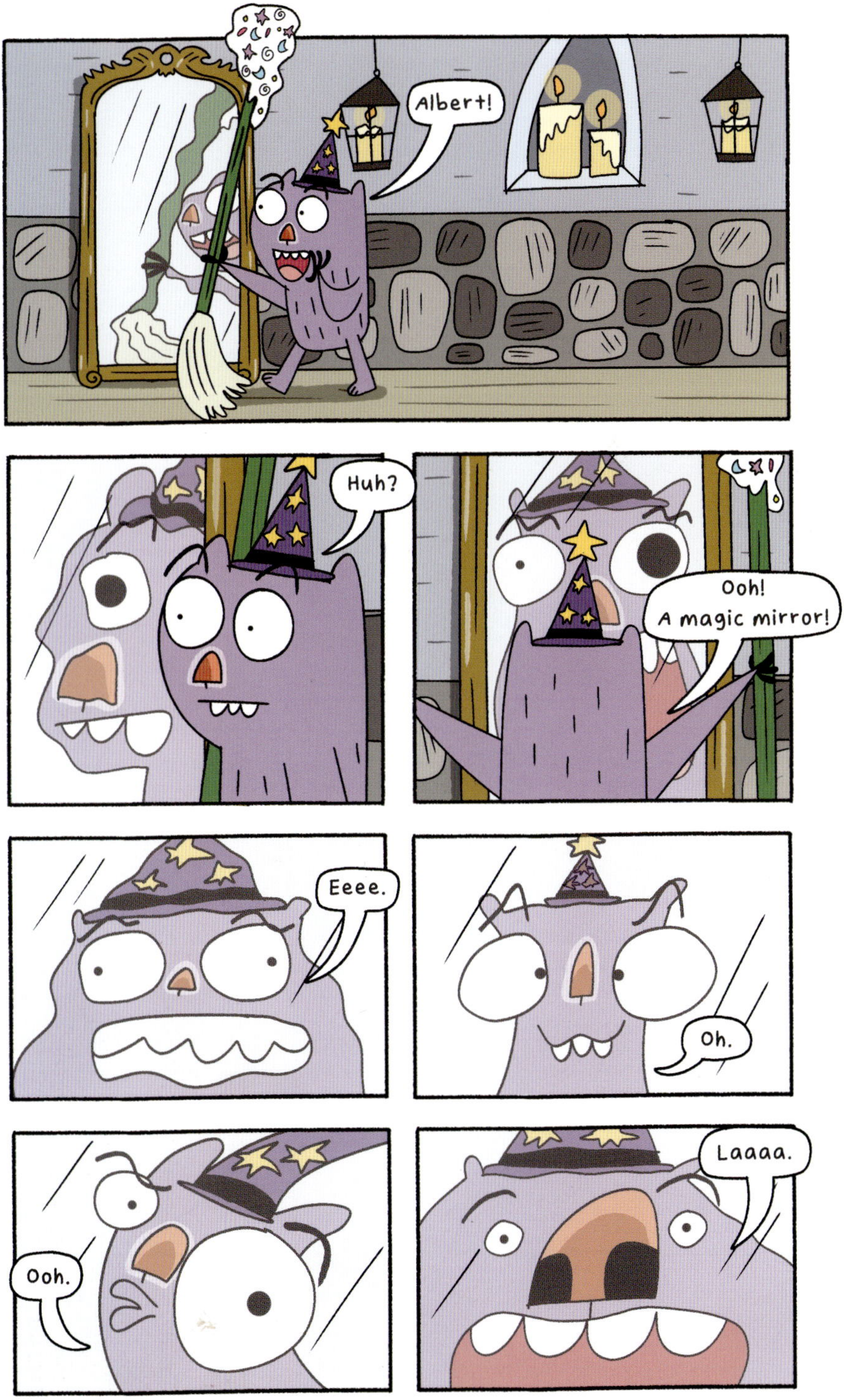
Albert!
Huh?
Ooh! A magic mirror!
Eeee.
Oh.
Ooh.
Laaaa.

Found a towel.
WEST WING
NORTH WING
Pickles?
Albert, I found a mop.
NORTH WING
Albert?

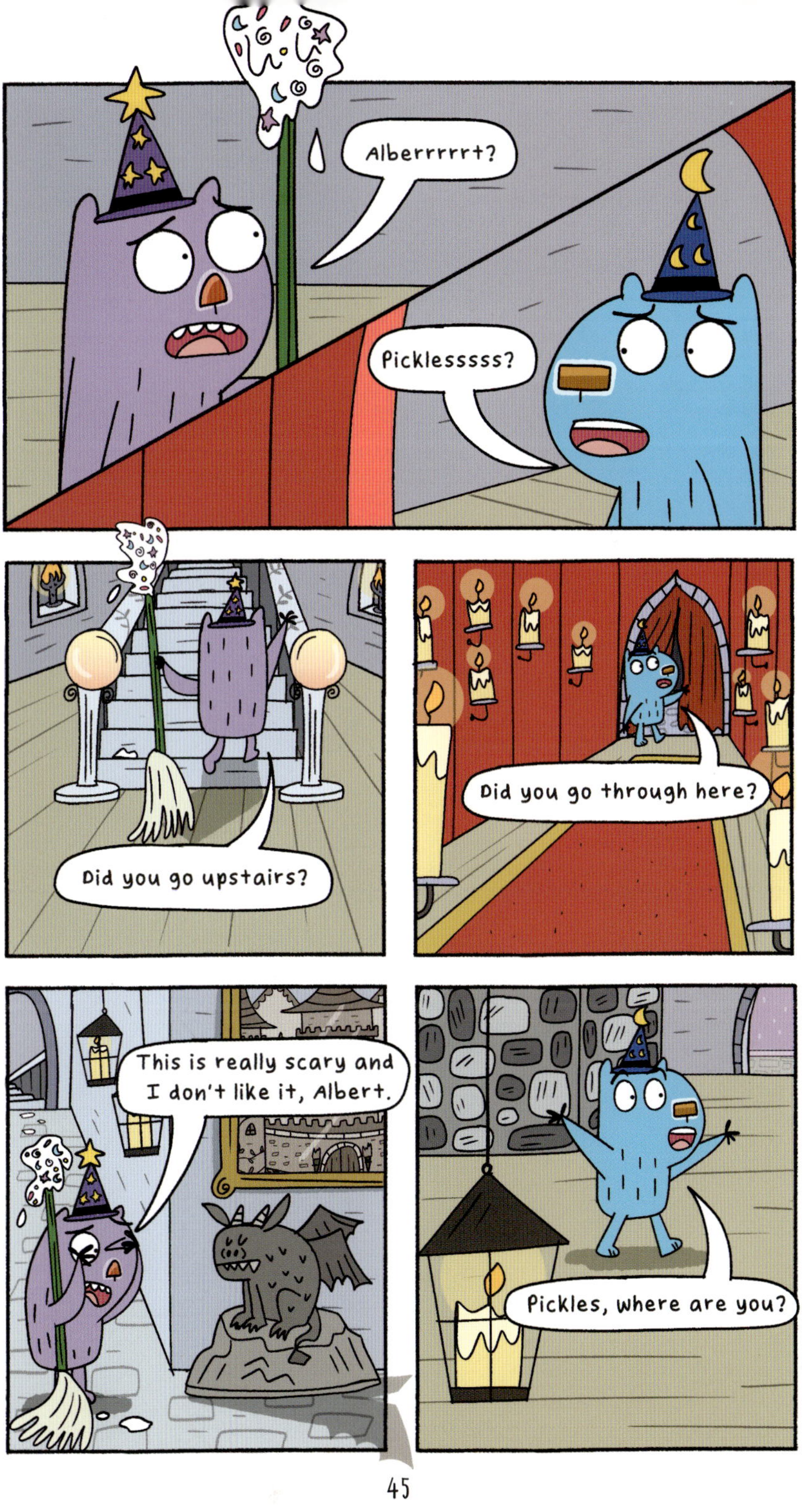
Alberrrrrt?
Picklesssss?
Did you go upstairs?
Did you go through here?
This is really scary and I don't like it, Albert.
Pickles, where are you?

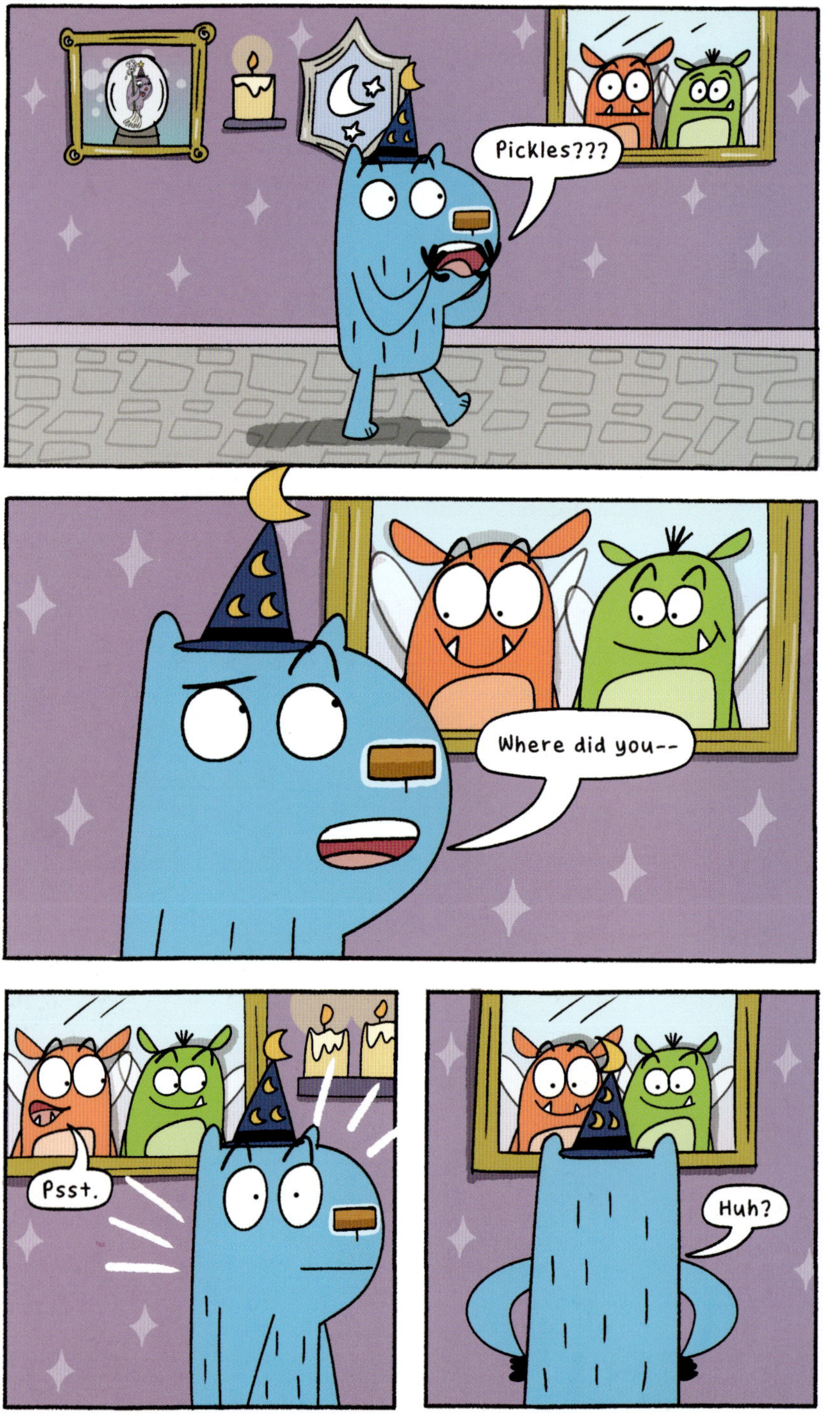
Pickles???
Where did you--
Psst.
Huh?

Hello!
Hello!
You look lost.
Must be some sort of interactive video...
Hey, where'd they go?

We can help you!
Yes! We can!
What are you two? Some sort of hologram?
What's a hologram? That sounds tasty.
So tasty!
No, we're BOUMs!
Bums?

No, BOUMs. B-O-U-M.
It stands for Beings of UneXplained Magic. But you can call me Tom.
Phil.
We're best BOUMs!
I feel like I'm stuck in a weird dream.

So are you?

In a weird dream? Apparently, if I'm talking to two--

BOUMs!

No, I mean are you lost?

I'm not, but my friend Pickles definitely is.

Short. Purple. Dripping Whimsy Whip everywhere.

Probably making this face.

I haven't seen a Pickles. Have you, Phil?
Negative.
You know, one time I couldn't find Phil. Do you remember that?
I do. We were in the crystal maze and it was summer. Hot. Really sunny.
Where is this going?
Well, one minute we were exploring the maze, and the next, Phil was gone.
Gone!

Phil? Where are ya, buddy?
Then I thought about how Phil has sensitive eyes.
Very sensitive.
Ow, my eyes.
So you know what I did next?
The suspense is killing me.
I went straight to the gift shop and there he was!
He needed sunglasses.
Still got 'em too.

That's a great story. But I need to find my friend.
Wait!
You missed the POINT of the story.
That Phil likes to shop?
That Tom knew where to find me because he knows me AND my sensitive eyeballs.
You guys are making my brain hurt. But actually, you may have a point.
Because we're smart!
So smart!

Albert?
Are you in here?
Ooh, potions.
And a wizard's robe.
Hey, it fits!
I AM THE MAJESTIC WIZARD OF WHIMSY WHIP.

AND NOW I WILL MAKE A MAGICAL POTION BECAUSE--
DO NOT PRESS
Um...
BECAUSE I AM MAGICAL!
I wonder what this does?
DO NOT PRESS

POOF
DO NOT PRESS
Cough, cough. ALBERT!
DO NOT PRESS
I CAN'T SEE MY HANDS!
I CAN'T SEE MY FEET!

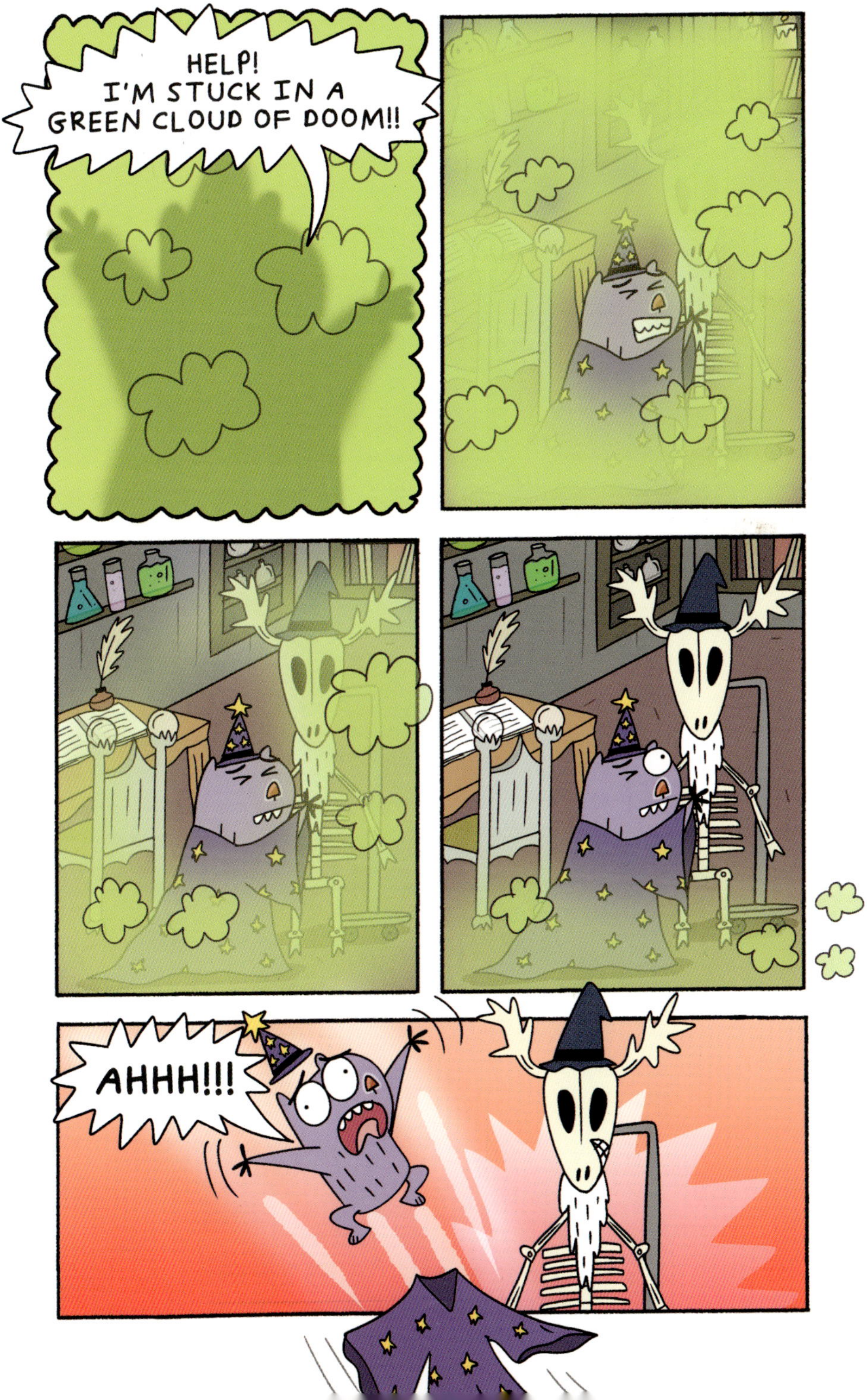
HELP!
I'M STUCK IN A
GREEN CLOUD OF DOOM!!
AHHH!!!

WIZARD'S CHAMBER
GET ME OUTTA HERE!
HUFF-PUFF-HUFF-PUFF.
HUG THE KITTY AND OPEN SESAME
I do NOT like skeletons.
HUG THE KITTY
AND OPEN SESAME

Hey, I didn't know wizards liked stuffed animals.
HUG THE KITTY
This kitty is so cute.
SQUEEZE
Meow.
CREEEAK
A magic stuffed kitty!
Hello?

Pickles wouldn't have waited for me here because... well, because Pickles doesn't stay still for very long.
Hey, Phil, have you ever had a Whimsy Whip before? They're really good. Try it.
Oh wow, that is good. Fruity.
EAST WING
WEST WING
NoRTH WING
YES! The drips. Good job, bums.
It's BOUMs!

Cough, cough.
The potion room.
Do you think something exploded?
Hmmm...
DO NOT PRESS
Yes. And I know who created the explosion.
Who?
DO NOT PRESS
Pickles.
My friend we're trying to find.
Are you paying any attention at all?

Pickles would have pressed this because...
DO NOT PRESS
Well, because it says not to.
Then Pickles would have freaked out in the green foggy clouds...
and flailed and flailed until--
FLAIL
FLAIL
BUMP

Bumping into THIS!
You mean Fred?
We go way back.
Pickles would have said something like "GET ME OUTTA HERE!" and run into the next room.
Which brings us to the wizard's chamber.

What do you think Pickles did here?
Try on some hats?
Wow, pink is really your color.
You think so?
No. Pickles would have been too scared.
Scared enough to hide...
HUG THE KITTY
AND OPE SESAME

HUG THE KITTY
AND OPEN SESAME
Under the covers.
Then take a nap.
Can you move over? You're on my side.
No I'm not!
Aw, look at this fluffy kitty.

Let me see that.
I wuv you, kitty.
What's he doing?
Shh.
He's having a moment.
Hey, look!
CREEAK
Whoooooaaaa.

Hello?
Anyone down here?
Albert?
Hmm-hmm-hmm.
Humming to myself
so I don't get scared.
Ew, it's dusty down here.
ACHOO!
Ohmygosh.

Albert? Where are you?
Gonna keep singing because I'm in the dark...
And I just walked into a spiderweb.
Wait, this isn't a--
CLICK
Secret library?

Look at all these books.
MAGIC WANDS 101
Ooh.
Ha!
6,000 WIZARD JOKES
What's this one?
Dinnerrr partyyy.
HOW TO HOST A WIZARD DINNER PARTY
GRUMBLE

I wonder if this castle has a kitchen.
Hmm... What's this?
SLURP! A chicken drumstick!
DUNGEON
I bet THIS is where the kitchen is.

Look.
There's a light on down there.
Does anyone have a flashlight?
No. But we glow in the dark.
Weird.
It's a library.
Does Pickles like books?
WOMBATS!
Go Camping
Yes.
But I don't think Pickles has books on the brain.
Then...what?
What Pickles is ALWAYS thinking about...food.
HOW TO HOST A WIZARD DINNER PARTY

But which door did you choose?
Maybe you tried this one first.
Why do you think Pickles went in here?
Actually, never mind.
I think Pickles chose this door.
Trust me, you do NOT want to go in there.

Seems kinda dark for a kitchen.
Hey, wizard! You might want to think about adding more lights!
And maybe a cozy breakfast nook.
There's gotta be some grub around here somewhere.
GASP!!

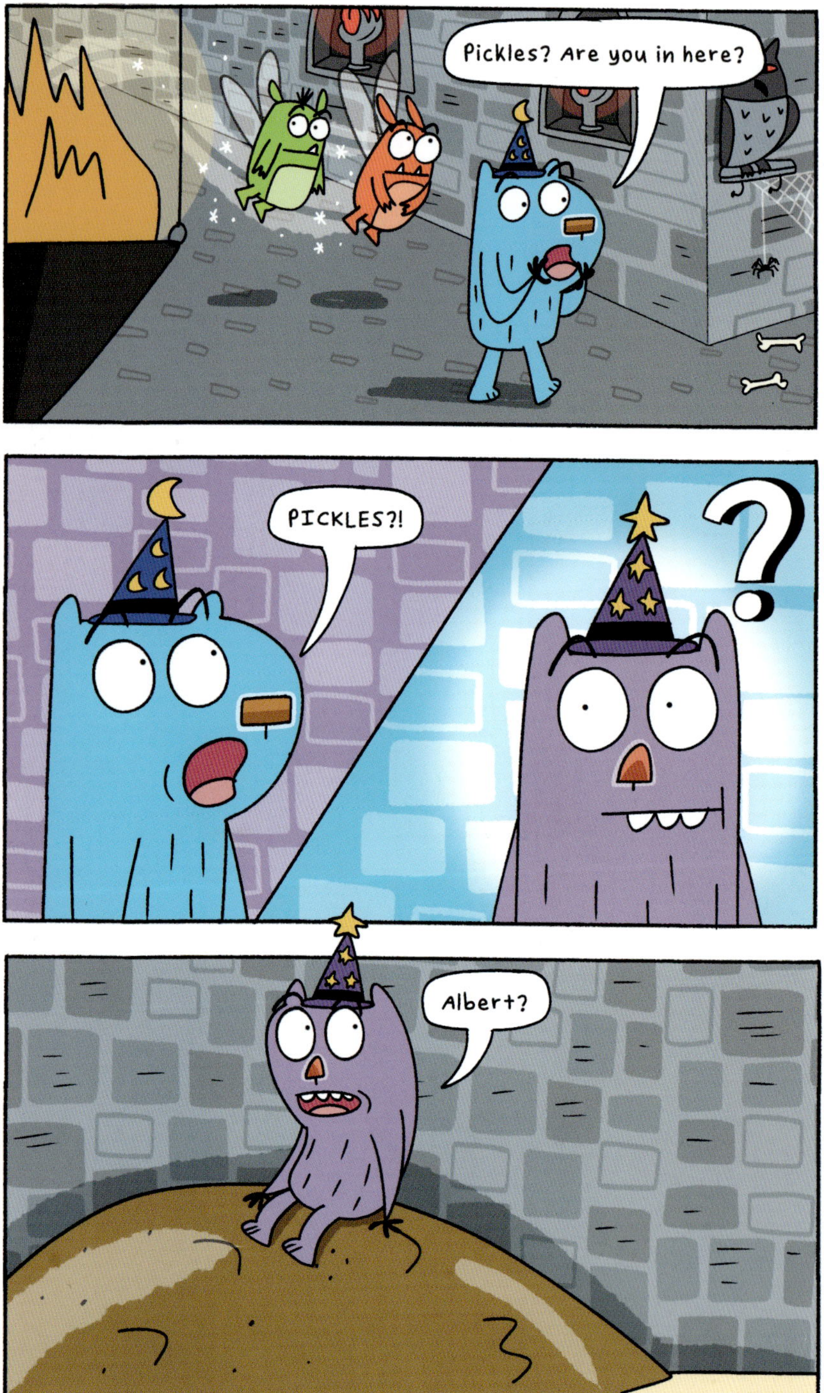
Pickles? Are you in here?
PICKLES?!
?
Albert?

ALBERT!!!
ALBERT! I'M OVER HERE!!!
Yeah, I know.
FLUFFY
Albert!
It's really you!
Are you okay?
No! I'm starving! But guess what! This chicken drummy is FAKE. Just like you said.
FLUF

It's a prop. Remember? This isn't a real wizard's castle.

FLUFFY

Why would a fake drummy be in a fake castle?

I have no idea. Ask Tom and Phil.

Who?

Where did they go?

Are you feeling okay? Maybe we should get you to a doctor.

Never mind. Let's get back to the entrance of the castle. Platters should be back by now.

STOP RIGHT THERE, YOU MINUSCULE MARSUPIALS.

IT IS I. THE GREAT AND POWERFUL WIZARD. AND YOU ARE TRESSPASSING IN MY CASTLE.

We can explain, Mr. Wizard, sir. You see, our friend Platters--
SILENCE!!!
Also, Mr. Wizard, do you have any real chicken drumsticks?
I SAID SILENCE!

We were just about to leave.
MUAHAHAHA. THERE IS ONLY ONE WAY OUT OF HERE.
And good luck, because you'll have to escape...
THE DRAGON!

What is THAT?!
I think the way out! Quick! Get in!
WHAT?!
It will be okay. Trust me.
Gulp.

When is it gonna move?
Will it go fast?
I don't want to go upside down!!
Hey, it's still not moving.
WHOOSH
AHH!!! It's moving!!!
Hold on!

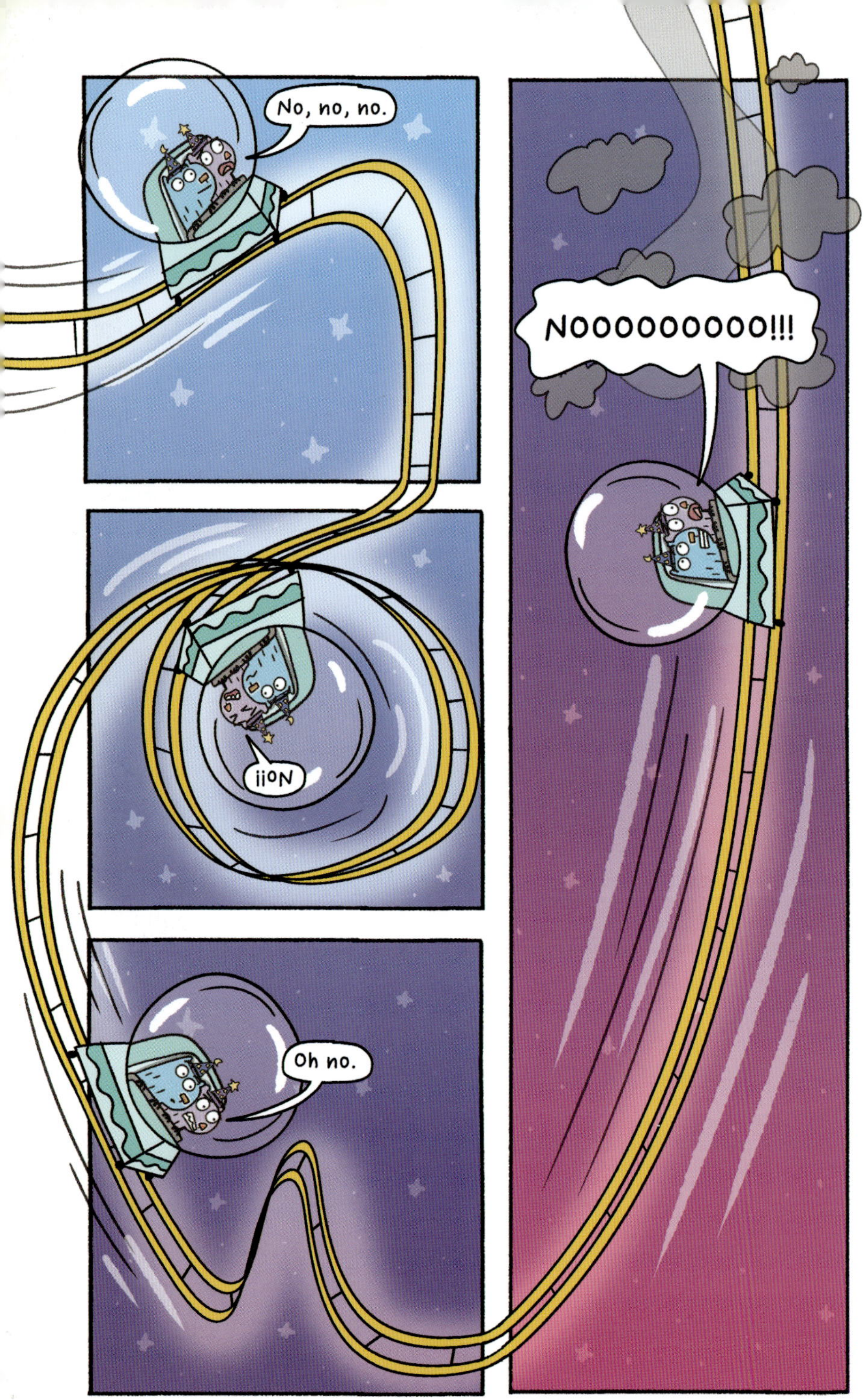
No, no, no.
No!!
Oh no.
NOOOOOOOOO!!!

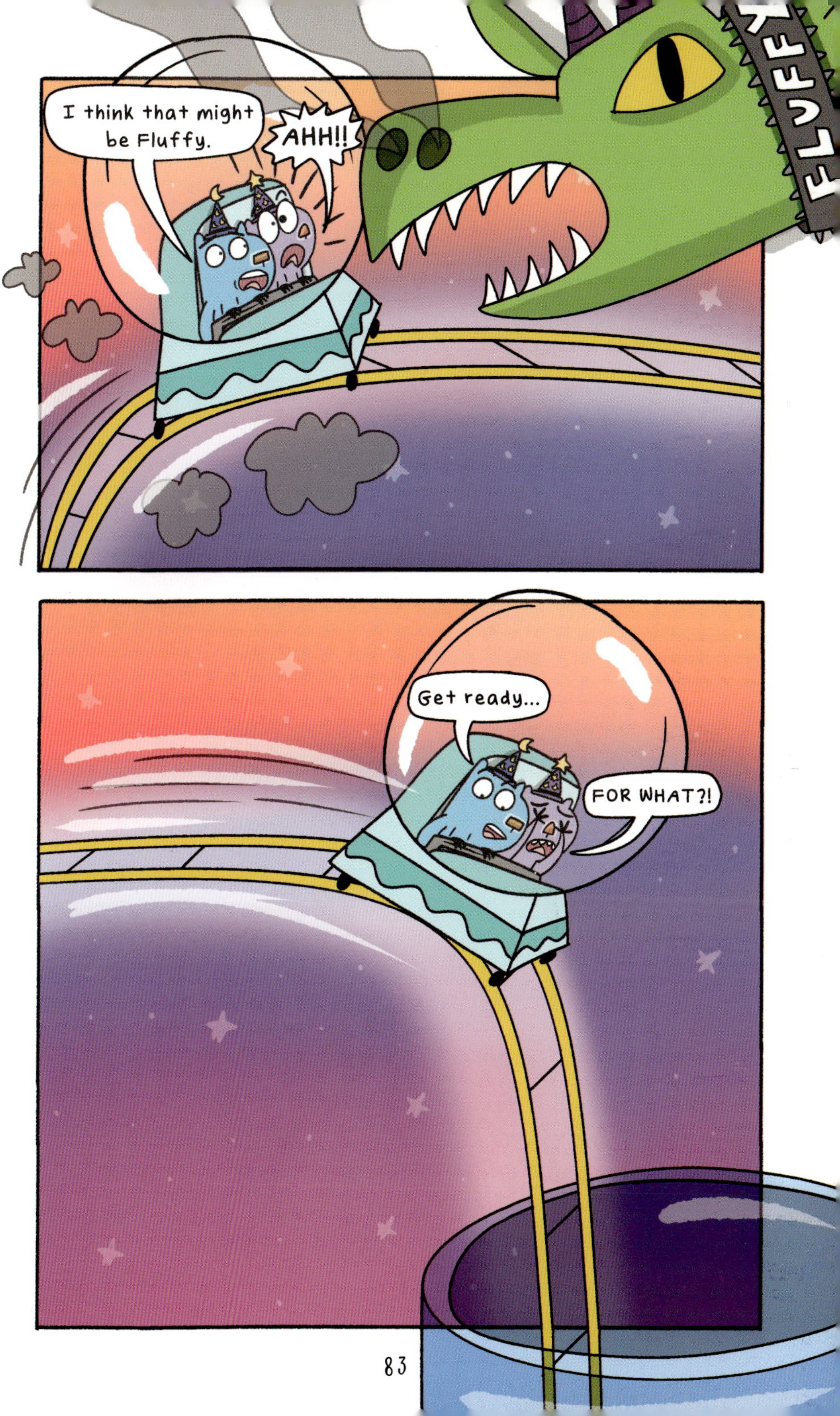
I think that might be Fluffy.
AHH!!
FLUFFY
Get ready...
FOR WHAT?!

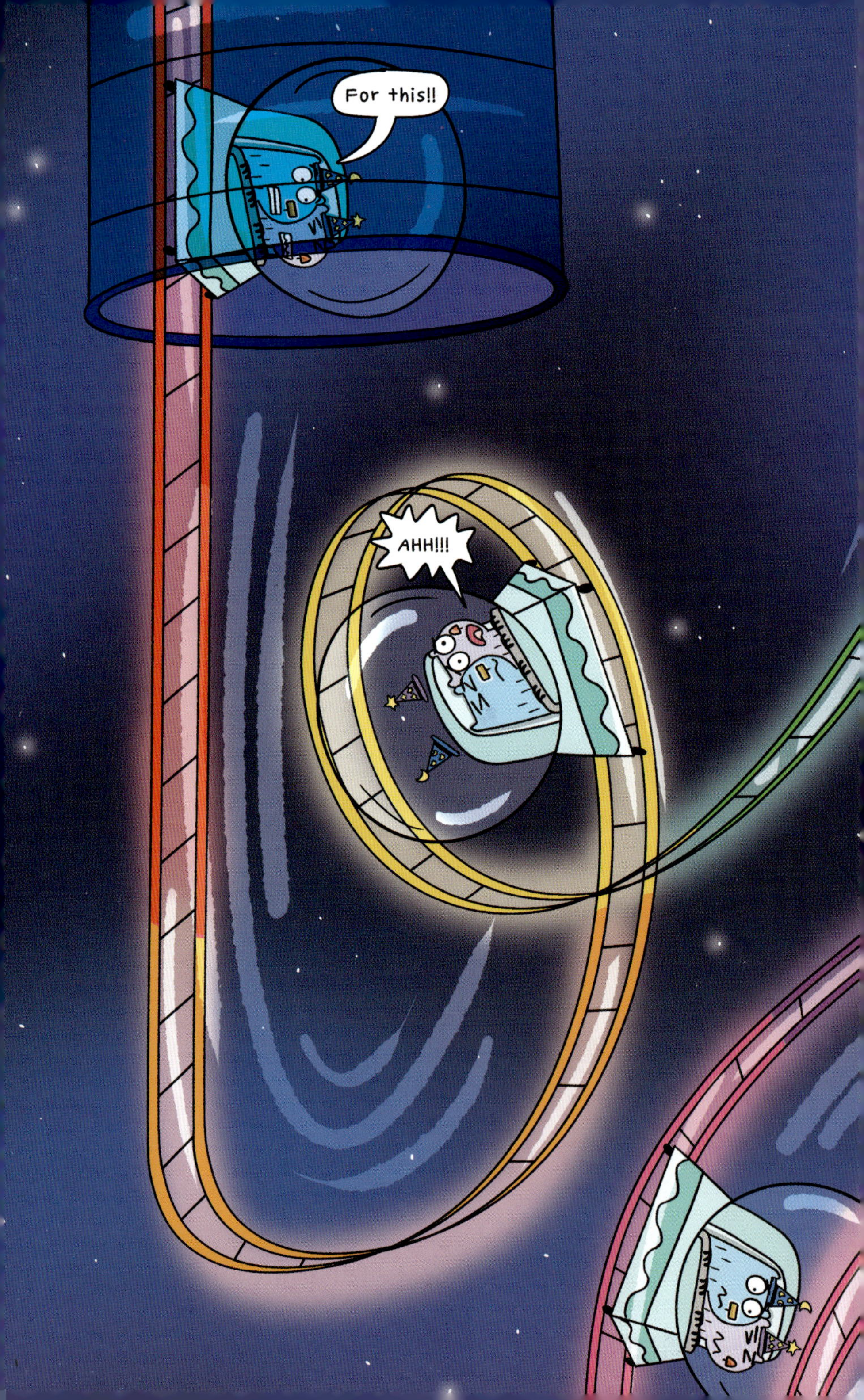
For this!!
AHH!!!

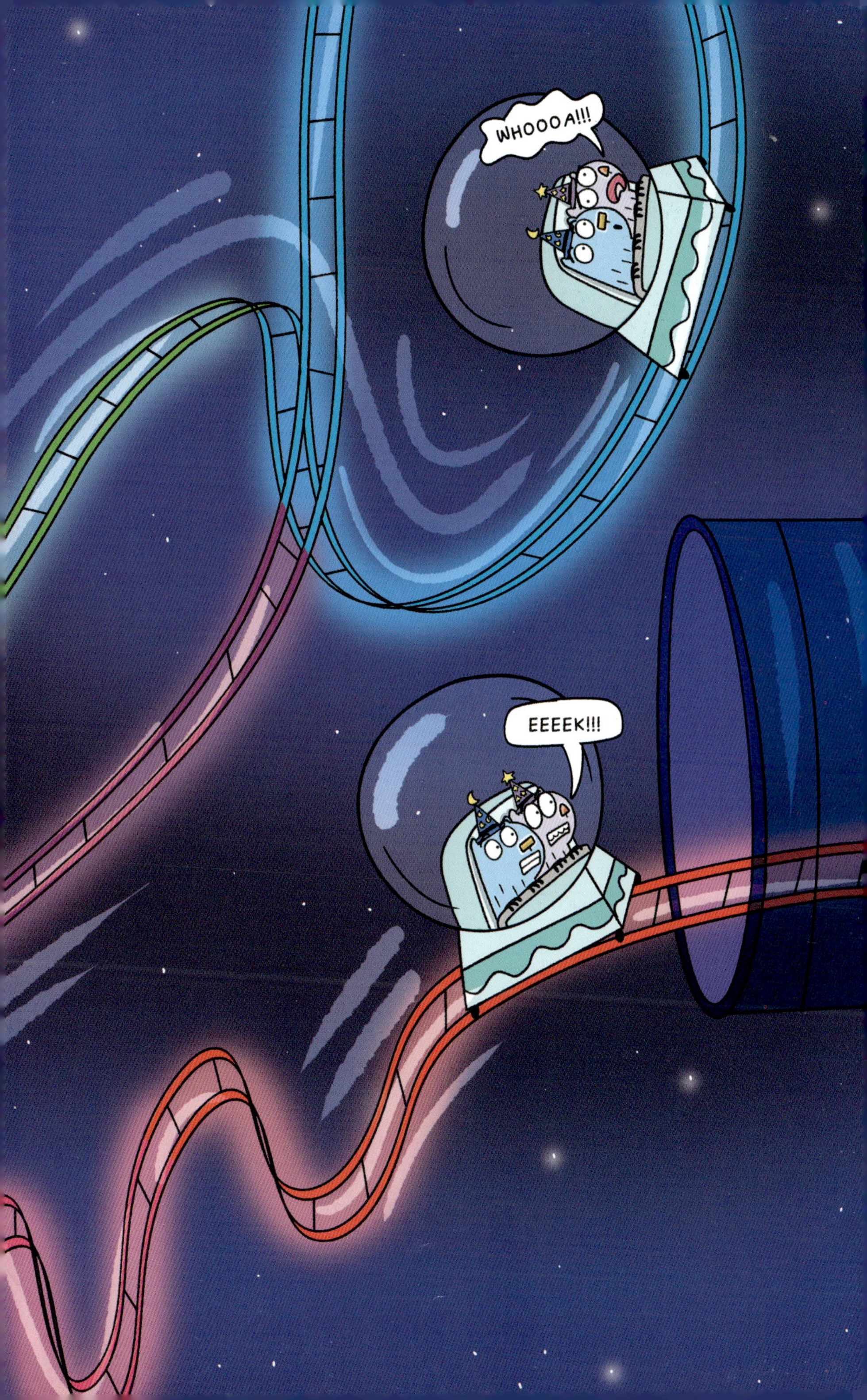
WHOOOA!!!
EEEEK!!!

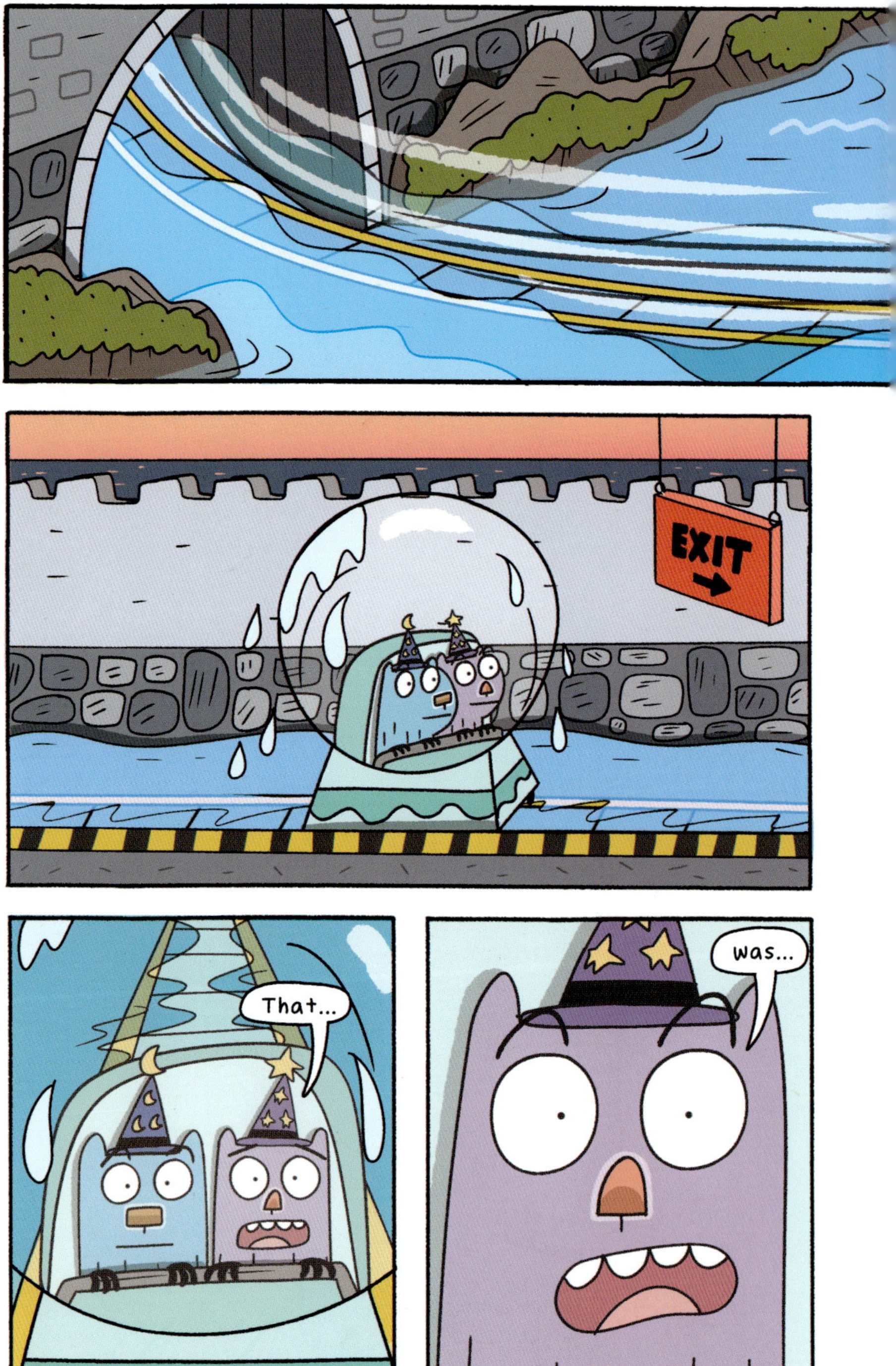
EXIT
That...
was...

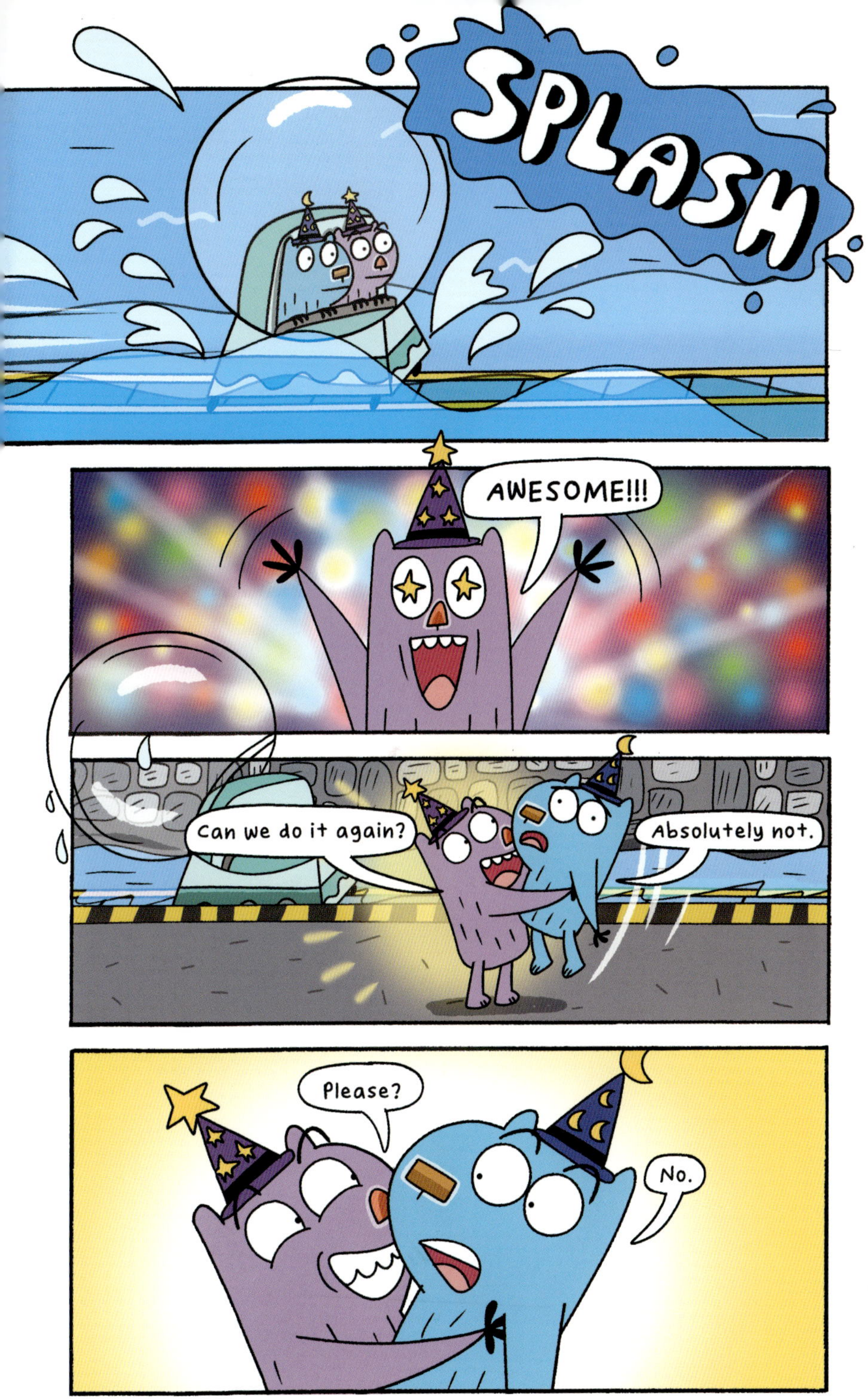
SPLASH
AWESOME!!!
Can we do it again?
Absolutely not.
Please?
No.

Hang on, wombats! I'm here!
How long before she notices?
Over here, Platters!
Huh?
PLATTERS •RMM•
Hey, you made it out! Sorry I took so long. The centaur swings broke down.
PLATTERS •RMM•

So what'd ya guys think?
It was so cool! Except for the scary parts.
What's the deal with the BOUMs? Phil and Tom?
Who and whose bums?
He bumped his head.
I swear they were real! Little magic fairy monsters!
GASP!!!

Did you just say...
Magic?
You definitely said magic.
What? No.
PLATTERS
YOU DID!!!
CYCLOPS
ARCADE
THE GRIFFIN GRILL
HEY, EVERYONE!
ALBERT BELIEVES IN MAGIC!

YE OLDE
DRUMMY HUT
MENU
BBQ
BUFFALO
TERIYAKI
Well, kids, I gotta get back to work, but these are on the house.
PLATTERS
Chickennnnn drummyyyy.
YUM YUM
So, Albert, how did you find me anyway?
I dunno, I went with my gut.

I love going with my gut!
CHOMP
BLACKSMITH
BAKERY
THE CAT'S MEOW
CAT SHOP
Shh. Fairies Sleeping
You know what the most magical thing of all is?
What?
Having you as my BFF.
AWW, Pickles.

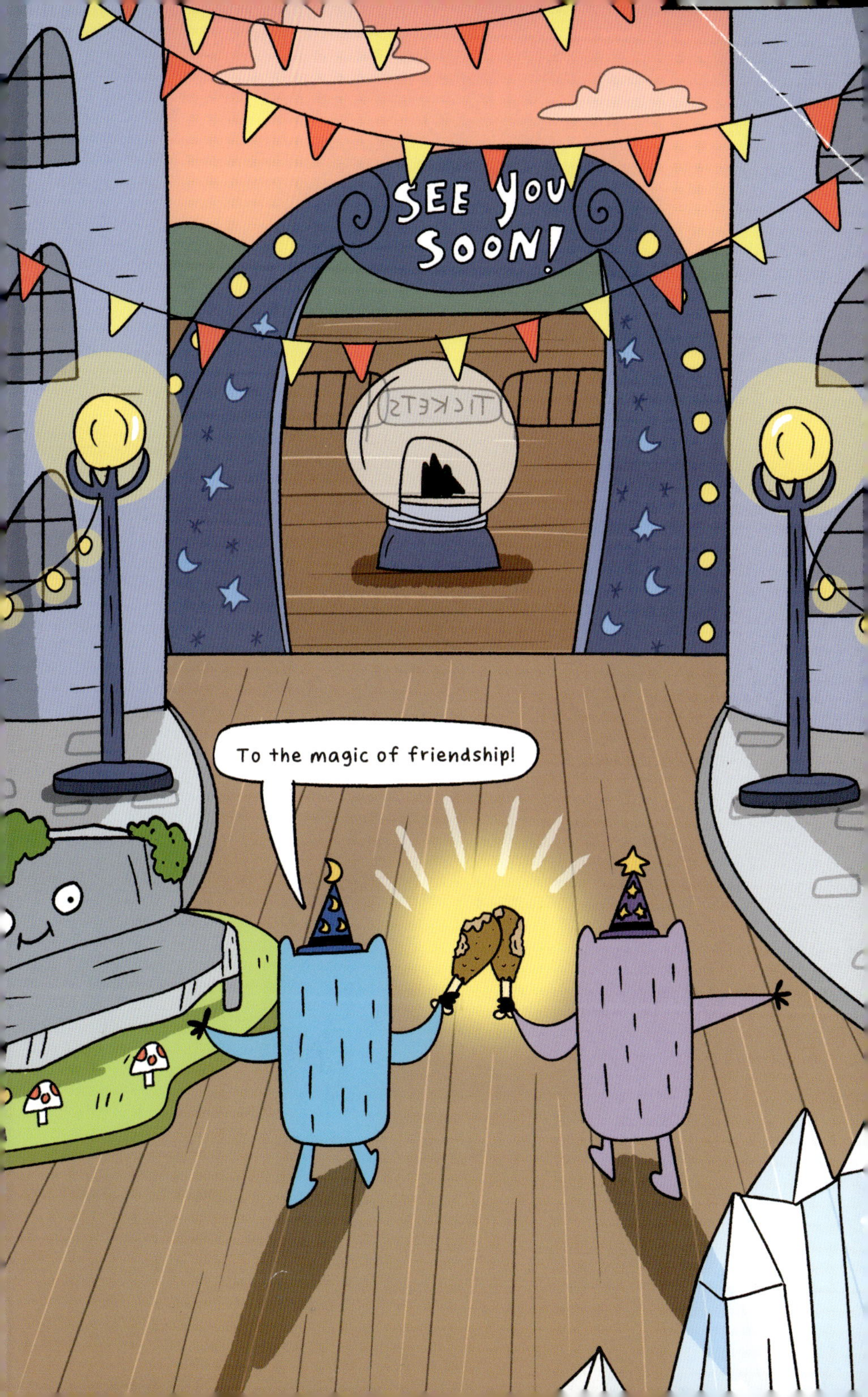
SEE YOU SOON!
To the magic of friendship!

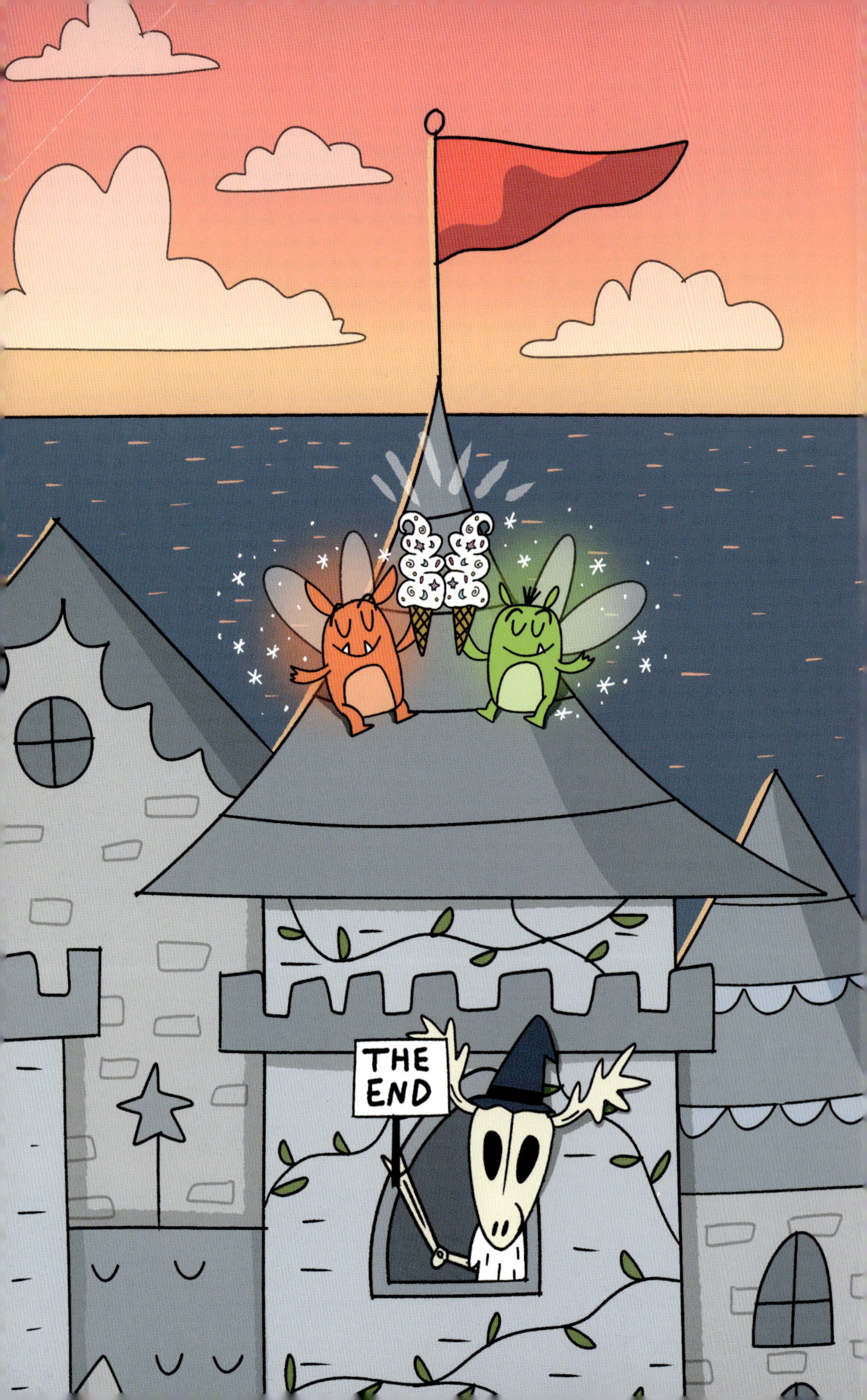
THE END

About the Author

Maddie Frost is the (maybe-someday award-winning) author-illustrator of several picture books, like *Smug Seagull*, *Just Be Jelly*, *Wakey Birds*, *Capybara Is Friends with Everyone*, *Iguana Be a Dragon*, and more.

She is a true believer in magic, especially in the magic of books!

Maddie lives in Massachusetts with her family. Visit her online at Maddie-Frost.com.

VIKING

An imprint of Penguin Random House LLC, New York

First published in the United States of America by Viking,
an imprint of Penguin Random House LLC, 2024

Copyright © 2024 by Maddie Frost

Penguin supports copyright. Copyright fuels creativity, encourages diverse voices, promotes free speech, and creates a vibrant culture. Thank you for buying an authorized edition of this book and for complying with copyright laws by not reproducing, scanning, or distributing any part of it in any form without permission. You are supporting writers and allowing Penguin to continue to publish books for every reader.

Viking & colophon are registered trademarks of Penguin Random House LLC.
The Penguin colophon is a registered trademark of Penguin Books Limited.

Visit us online at PenguinRandomHouse.com.

Library of Congress Cataloging-in-Publication Data is available.

ISBN 9780593465424

10 9 8 7 6 5 4 3 2 1

Manufactured in China

TOPL

Book design by Maddie Frost   Typeset in Delivery Note and Lets Draw Fun Animals Bold
The illustrations in this book were created with Procreate.

This book is a work of fiction. Any references to historical events, real people, or real places are used fictitiously. Other names, characters, places, and events are products of the author's imagination, and any resemblance to actual events or places or persons, living or dead, is entirely coincidental.

The publisher does not have any control over and does not assume any responsibility for author or third-party websites or their content.

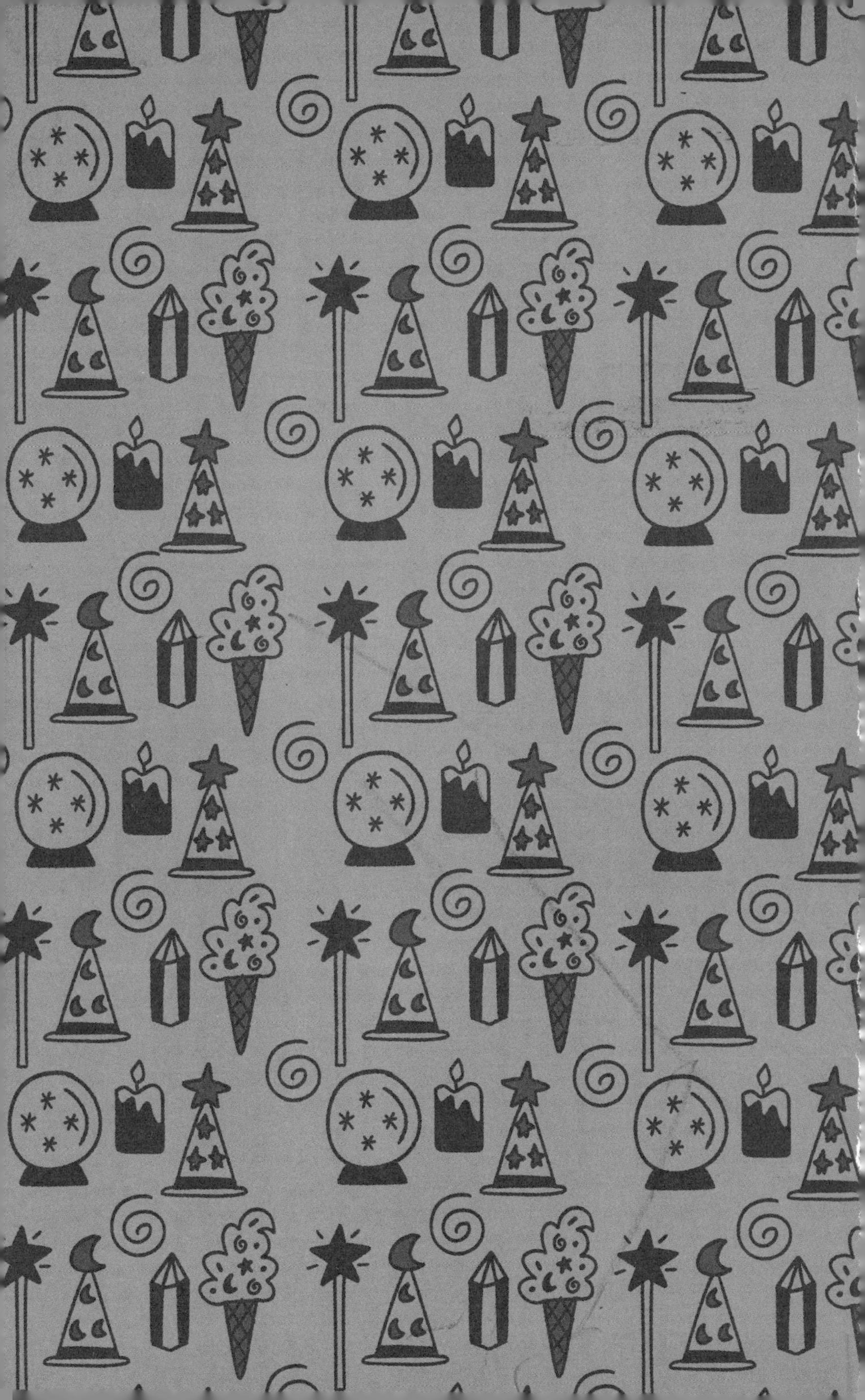

SCJC

MAR -- 2024

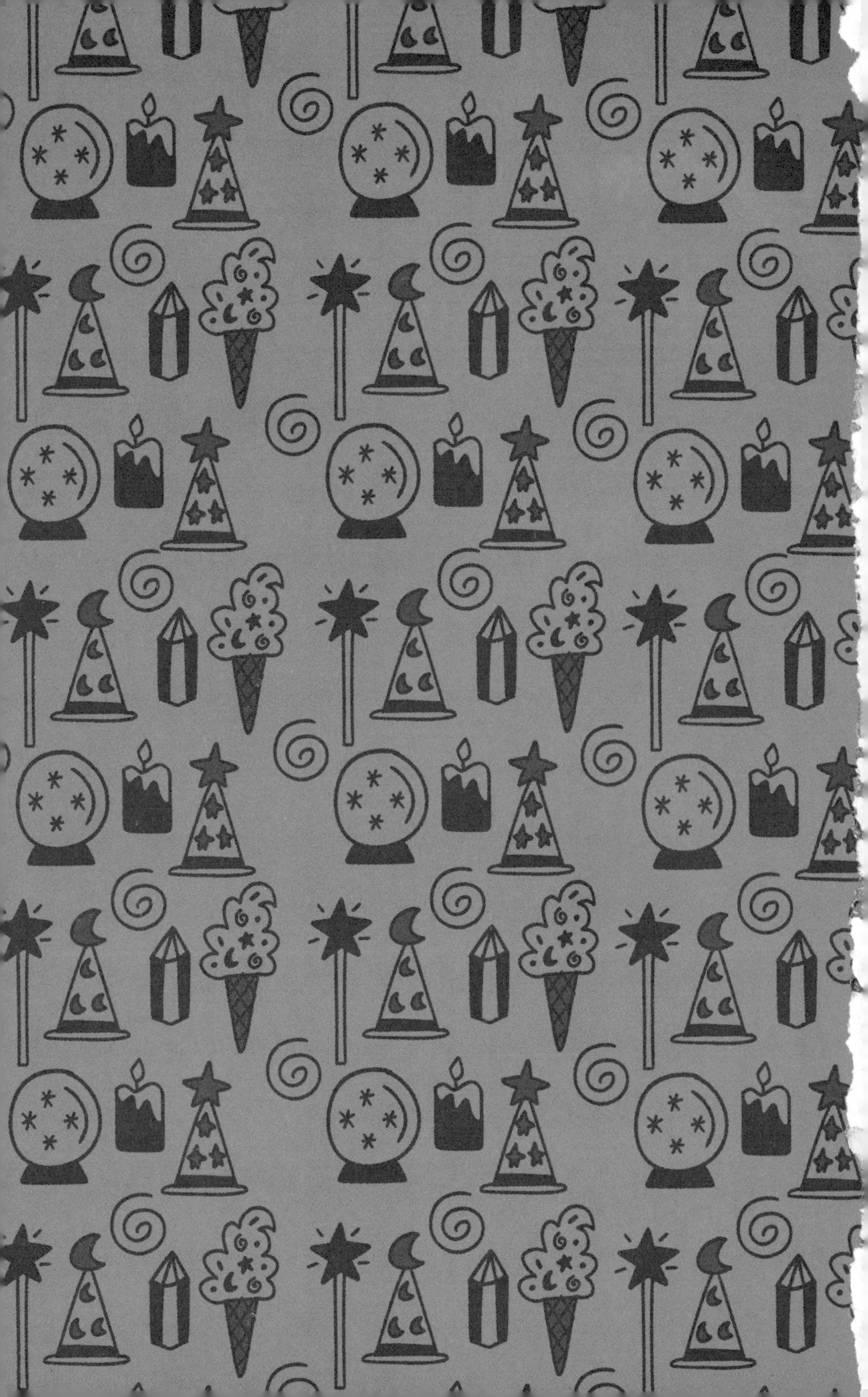